This book is dedicated to
my little sloth lover Maddie.

"A Sloth Life"
written and illustrated by Amy Hammond and Staci Talley.

"I Fell in Love With a Sloth"
written by Brandi Lewis.

"Ozzy & Me: In Quarantine"
written by Brandi Lewis.

"The Magic Sloth"
written by Brandi Lewis.

Bonus Story, "My Friend Karen"
written by Brandi Lewis and illustrated by Margaret Warren.

A SPECIAL NOTE OF THANKS:

Thank you Anand and team for making this happen!
Thank you Staci and Amy for the collaborative efforts.
Thank you Margaret, my dearest childhood friend, for joining me on
the bonus story "My Friend Karen."
Thank you to Mom, Maddie, Abby, and Charlie being such great models!
A shout out to the beautiful communities of Clinton and Shirley.

Table Of Contents

Sloth Stories:

Section 1

Printed in the United States of America.
Copyright © 2020 by Be Bold Retail LLC
All rights reserved.

Published By: Be Bold Retail LLC
ISBN: 978-0-578-69639-3

A SLOTH'S LIFE

written and illustrated by Amy Hammond and Staci Talley.

Good morning, New York City!
Snax is waking from a dream.
Time for all you sloths to rise –
of every fur and shape and size.

Today: a sloth-y shower.
Snax's fur made soft and clean.
Then a brushing of the teeth.
He tucks his slippers underneath.

Who has the whitest smile?
SNAX! And it's no wonder.
He brushes every single inch.
It's a habit; it's a cinch.

So many choices. What to wear?
He's stylish in the City.
Another day, another hood –
a sunny yellow's always good!

Earbuds in and backpack on:
There's no time left to waste.
"I'm coming; I'll be right there!"
He slides into a kitchen chair.

Time to pack a healthy snack.
Snax picks a favorite bag.
He counts: eight, nine, ten berries.
Four – no five – perfect cherries.

A subway stop is steps away.
He would rather walk.
The train roars beneath his feet.
Snax makes his way across the street.

**This is Public School 901.
All his friends are waiting:
There's Sporty Sofie, Turbo Tad.
Artsy Annie and Mr. McGrad.**

Each one has a special gift –
so the teacher tells them.
Snax always takes his time.
It's a superpower, not a crime.

A sloth sees things that others don't.
Like ants that scuttle up a hill.
How many of them? Lots.
He counts a ladybug's perfect dots.

After math comes history,
and then his favorite subject.
Snax finds the word that's
spelled wrong.
His eye to detail's very strong.

What's inside the lunchbox?
Snax packed it full of care.
Fruit and nuts – a special treat!
Healthy food he likes to eat.

Why can't school be longer?
Snax sighs. It's almost over.
Weekdays are way too short.
Now time to build a secret fort.

High-fives all around!
He'll see his friends tomorrow.
The sun begins to set.
Snax is the happiest a City sloth
can get.

I Fell in Love With A Sloth

He finally arrives!

Written by Brandi Lewis

I have always loved my stuffed animal friends.

I share my friends with Memaw sometimes. After all, they are good company.

Sometimes Memaw doesn't think she needs that much company.

I have 5 bears,
5 bunnies,
4 puppies, 3 cats,
2 pigs, 2 monkeys,
an elephant, a lion,
a moose, a mammoth,
a penguin, a seal,
a red panda ...
and more.
I love them ALL.

Mom said I have too
many...

So you can imagine my surprise when Mom told me I was getting a sloth!

I could hardly wait!

But I did wait.

Every day, I sat here, waiting for the special delivery.

I wanted my new friend that would respond to me and talk back to me. I needed my Snax the Sloth!

Bark bark bark!

"Charlie, it's ok,
it's my sloth!
My sloth is finally
here!" I cheer.

I rush out to see.

I peer outside,
I see the box.
It could be my sloth.
My sloth could fit in
that box.

WOW!!!
I press his hand and say, "I love you."
He slowly responds...

"I   L ooooooo ve

youuuuuuuuuu!"

We call up his friends to share our good news.

Welcome home
Ozzy!

Written by Brandi Lewis

We swing!

We dance.

One day, we fell into a trance.

Being Quarantined
is hard. I tell Mommy
I miss my friends.

Ozzy says
"IIIIIIIIIIIIIIIIIIIIIII
mmmiiiiiiiiiiiiiissssss
mmmmmyyyyyyyy
frrieeeeeennndss".

Ozzy and me, we are in this together.

We wash our hands.
I sing my Abc's.
Ozzy says Aaaa,
Bbbbbb.....

I could be
washing my hands
for awhile...

We go on bike rides together. I say to Ozzy as we fly down the trail, "WEEEEEeeee".

Ozzy says to me, "WEEEeeeeee" so I know he's having fun too.

It's good to have Ozzy by my side.

The Magic Sloth

written by Brandi Lewis

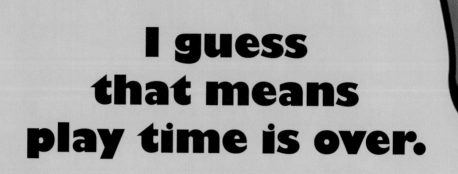

Pooof!!! Hi!

WOW! Who are you?

We can work as a team!

"Honey, is your room clean?"

"Yes Mom, my sloth helped me!"

"Oh ok sweetie. Well thank you for cleaning your room."

"Hee, hee... Shhhh!! Don't tell, maybe your sloth has magic too!

My Friend Karen

written by Brandi Lewis and illustrated by Margaret Warren.

Karen lives next door to me. Karen and I play a lot because she is my neighbor.

She has a lot
of opinions.

Me: I like your
pink hat.

Karen: It's fuchsia.

Karen: Cats DO NOT meow. They purr.

Me: Cats definitely meow! Are you teasing me? Humph

It can be
frustrating being
Karen's friend.

Whenever we play dolls, it seems like Karen always INSISTS she be the princess.

Sometimes we agree to disagree!

Sometimes Karen

likes to tell me
what to do...

...and she's not always "wrong".

And sometimes she's a lot of fun. When we play Red Light, Green Light, we make up lights like orange light. That means turn around. Yellow light means move forward very slowly; pink light means back up. Blue light means tickle and purple light means hug!

Sometimes Karen joins us for lunch. She likes her bread toasted, but not too toasted. She can't eat lettuce and she doesn't like her vegetables. She doesn't want her hot dog boiled or grilled, only microwaved will do. She doesn't like lemonade if it's too sweet or too sour. She only likes fruit if it's just the RIGHT amount of ripeness.

If her ice melts, she needs a new cup. An entirely new cup!

One day I wore mismatched socks by mistake. Some kids were laughing at me. Karen stood up for me and said, "Oh no, is it mismatched sock day today? I totally forgot! "

Yes, I'm here.

Mom says it is good to have all kinds of friends. We are all different and it would be nice if we could learn to like each other despite our differences.

Karen and I do lots of fun things to-gether. We bike to school together almost every day.

Of course, Karen insists she must always be in the lead.